The Tadpole Prince

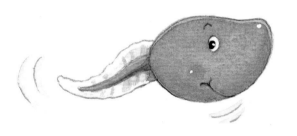

Nick Ward

Pavilion Children's
Books

I
n a quiet corner of the palace gardens, deep in a still green pond, a little tadpole popped out of his egg...

POP!

"Wow!" he gasped as he saw all the wonderful creatures swimming around him.

"What will I be when I grow up?"

"What will I be when I grow up?" he asked
a wise old fish. "Will I be as big and brave as you?"
"What's the hurry?" smiled the wise old fish.
"Anything may happen. Just wait and see!"

So the impatient little tadpole waited ...

and waited ...

until one day...

"Well, who would have guessed!" croaked the little frog,
jumping onto a lily-pad. "I'm a fr–"

But just then a passing princess scooped him up.

"Are you my handsome prince?" she asked, giving him a kiss.

"Oh dear," said the little frog, feeling another change coming on...

A naughty fairy grabbed the princess and whisked her away to a tall rickety tower.

"Help!" she cried. "Save me!"

So the handsome prince ran through the woods and over a mountain, till he came to the tall rickety tower.

But two ugly trolls were guarding the tower.

"**Gnarr!**" they roared, scrunching up their faces.

"That's not scary," said the handsome prince. And he pulled such horrible faces that the trolls screamed and ran away!

So the handsome prince rescued the princess, which turned him into a...

POP!

Hero! "You're my hero!" sighed the princess, and the hero quickly marched the Big Bad Wolf and some big bully giants out of town. (That was a hero's job, you see.)

"And don't come back till you're sorry!" he ordered.

Hands OFF! B.B.W.

The princess was so grateful to him for making her country safe that she decided to marry her hero. And this turned him into a rich and powerful...

King! He was a kind and considerate king and was loved by all his subjects, right down to the lowliest pig farmer. They lived in a beautiful palace and were very happy together.

Soon the king and queen had a baby daughter,
and this turned the king into a...

Daddy! "Yippee, I'm a daddy!" He was
so excited that he held a huge party.

Everyone was invited:
the Three Bears,
the Three Little Pigs
and Little Red Riding Hood.

To the baby

Everyone except the naughty fairy!

The naughty fairy was so annoyed that she
wrapped a wicked magic spell in a box, and tied
a beautiful bow on top. "I'll teach him!" she grumbled.

The naughty fairy put on a disguise
and took her present to the king...

"Congratulations!" she cackled.
But the king recognized the fairy
and guessed it was a trick.

Toot!
Toot!

Squeak

"I can't undo the bow," he pretended.

"Oh, give it here, silly!" said the naughty fairy.

Fizz

And she ripped off the paper and opened the box.
"Oh no!"

The magic spell whizzed around the fairy's head and -POP!- she disappeared.

POP!

"Where has she gone?" cried the king.

In a quiet corner of the palace gardens, deep in a still green pond, a naughty little tadpole gasped at all the wonderful creatures.

POP!

"What will I be when I grow up?"
she wondered...